This edition published by Parragon Books Ltd in 2015

Parragon Books Ltd
Chartist House
15–17 Trim Street
Bath BA1 1HA, UK
www.parragon.com

ISBN 978-1-4748-1984-8

Printed in China

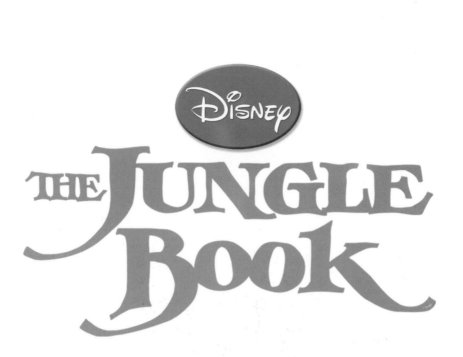

Bath · New York · Cologne · Melbourne · Delhi
Hong Kong · Shenzhen · Singapore · Amsterdam

Long ago, deep in the jungles of India, there lived a wise and kind black panther named Bagheera. One day, as Bagheera walked along the river, he saw something surprising – a baby! The baby was lying in a boat that had crashed on to the shore.

'Why, it's a Man-cub!' the panther said to himself.

The Man-cub was in urgent need of food and care, but the closest Man-village was days away. So Bagheera took the baby to a nearby wolf family. The mother had just had pups, and Bagheera hoped she would accept the Man-cub as one of her own.

The panther placed the baby near the den and stepped away.
After a few quick sniffs, the mother wolf gently carried the baby
into her den. Bagheera's plan had worked!

For the next ten years, Mowgli, as the Man-cub came to be called, lived happily with the wolves. He quickly became a favourite amongst all the jungle animals. All, that is, except Shere Khan, a strong and cunning tiger.

Shere Khan feared nothing but Man's gun and Man's fire. He had heard of the young Man-cub and believed that Mowgli would grow up to be a hunter. The tiger wanted to make sure that did not happen.

One night, the wolf elders met at Council Rock to discuss the matter. Akela, the wolf leader, declared that, for everyone's safety, Mowgli would have to leave the pack.

'But the boy cannot survive alone in the jungle!' protested Mowgli's father, Rama.

Bagheera, who had returned often during the years to check on Mowgli, had been listening to the wolves.

He jumped down from his perch in the tree and approached Akela and Rama.

'Maybe I can help,' he said. 'I know a Man-village where Mowgli would be safe.'

'So be it,' said Akela. 'There is no time to lose. Good luck!'

Early the next morning, Bagheera and Mowgli set out. They travelled fast, and were soon deep in the jungle.

The two travelled well into the night. 'Bagheera,' said Mowgli, 'I'm getting sleepy. Shouldn't we start back home?'

Bagheera told Mowgli about Shere Khan and the wolf council's decision. Mowgli was shocked.

'I don't want to go to the Man-village!' he protested.

Bagheera promised Mowgli that things would seem better in the morning. He helped the Man-cub climb a tall tree. 'We'll be safer up here,' the panther said.

They settled down on a tree branch, and in no time at all Bagheera was sound asleep, while Mowgli brooded over his fate. Neither one noticed Kaa, the snake, slither towards Mowgli.

'Ssssay now, what have we here?' said Kaa. 'It's a Man-cub. A delicious Man-cub.'

Mowgli tried to shove Kaa out of his face. 'Oh, go away and leave me alone,' he said, annoyed.

Kaa refused to leave. He kept slithering towards Mowgli, and when Mowgli finally looked straight at Kaa, the snake used his eyes to put Mowgli into a trance.

Kaa coiled himself around Mowgli and was preparing to eat him! Suddenly, Bagheera woke up and saw what was happening.

Moving quickly, the panther slapped Kaa on the head. The snake released Mowgli from his grip.

An angry Kaa turned on Bagheera. However, before the snake could coil himself around Bagheera, Mowgli pushed him off the tree branch. A defeated and hungry Kaa slithered off into the jungle.

The next morning, Mowgli and Bagheera were awakened by a loud rumbling and shaking.

'A parade!' Mowgli shouted enthusiastically.

Bagheera covered his ears and groaned, 'Oh no, the dawn patrol again!'

Mowgli grabbed a vine and swung down from the tree to take a look.

Mowgli watched as a long line of elephants marched proudly along in single file. He hurried over to a baby elephant at the very end of the line.

'Can I join in?' asked Mowgli.

'Sure!' said the baby elephant. 'Just do what I do!'

Mowgli got in step behind the baby elephant and began to march along. Then he got down on all fours to walk more like the elephants in front of him.

Suddenly, Colonel Hathi, at the head of the line, called out, 'To the rear, march!'

Mowgli did not know that meant the entire company had to turn around. Whomp! He and the baby elephant bumped into each other.

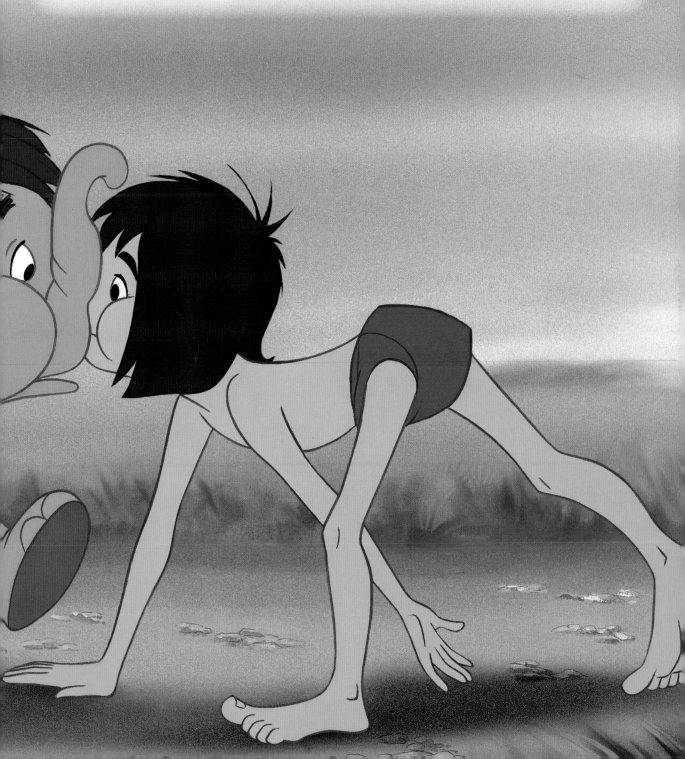

'Company, halt!' Colonel Hathi shouted, and all the elephants stopped and stood ready for inspection. Mowgli tried to fit in, but Colonel Hathi figured out that Mowgli was a Man-cub.

The Colonel lifted Mowgli high with his trunk. 'I'll have no Man-cub in my jungle!' he cried.

'This is not your jungle!' an offended Mowgli replied.

At that moment, Bagheera rushed over. 'The Man-cub is with me,' he told Colonel Hathi. 'I'm taking him to the Man-village.'

'To stay?' demanded Colonel Hathi.

'You have my word!' said Bagheera.

'Good!' said the elephant. 'And remember, an elephant never forgets!' With that, Colonel Hathi turned and marched off with his troop.

'You're going to the Man-village right now!' said Bagheera.

'I'm staying right here!' Mowgli cried. He wrapped his arms around a small tree.

'You're going if I have to drag you!' shouted Bagheera, and he tried, unsuccessfully, to pull Mowgli off the tree.

Bagheera lost his temper. 'From now on you're on your own!' he declared, and stalked off.

'Don't worry about me!' an equally angry Mowgli yelled after him.

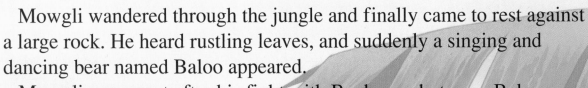

Mowgli wandered through the jungle and finally came to rest against a large rock. He heard rustling leaves, and suddenly a singing and dancing bear named Baloo appeared.

Mowgli was upset after his fight with Bagheera, but once Baloo arrived, it was hard to stay in a bad mood!

Baloo offered to teach Mowgli about the bare necessities of life in the jungle. He showed Mowgli how to find bananas, coconuts and other foods. He showed him how to scratch his back on a tree, too. The whole time, Baloo sang and danced. Mowgli couldn't help but smile and feel better.

The two new friends splashed and played in the river and then floated contentedly downstream together. Mowgli joined in as Baloo sang some more.

'I like being a bear!' said Mowgli.

'You're going to make one swell bear!' said Baloo. 'Why, you even sing like one!'

Suddenly, a group of monkeys swooped down
from the trees and grabbed Mowgli!
'Hey!' screamed Mowgli. 'Let go of me!'
He struggled against the monkeys, who just
chittered and laughed and held on to him.

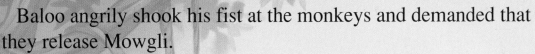

Baloo angrily shook his fist at the monkeys and demanded that they release Mowgli.

'Come on and get him!' taunted one of the monkeys.

The monkeys aimed a steady chorus of jeers and insults at Baloo. They aimed plenty of fruit at him, too!

The monkeys swung through the trees, tossing Mowgli along as they went. 'Baloo!' cried Mowgli. 'Help me! They're carrying me away.'

Baloo knew he needed Bagheera to help him. He called for the panther as loudly as he could. As soon as Bagheera heard Baloo's cries, he hurried towards the bear.

Baloo told Bagheera that the monkeys had carried Mowgli off. Bagheera figured that the monkeys were taking Mowgli to the ruins of an ancient city, where their ruler, an orangutan named King Louie, lived. Bagheera and Baloo set off at once to save Mowgli.

Meanwhile, while King Louie and the monkeys danced and sang, the King told Mowgli that he dreamed of being human. He had heard that Mowgli wanted to stay in the jungle and he offered to help the Man-cub. In return, the King wanted Mowgli to tell him the secret of how people made fire.

'But I don't know how to make fire,' Mowgli said. King Louie did not believe him.

Bagheera and Baloo arrived at the ruins in time to hear what King Louie wanted.

Bagheera quickly came up with a plan. 'While you create a disturbance,' he said to Baloo, 'I'll rescue Mowgli.'

Baloo disguised himself as an ape and burst in to join the dancing. King Louie took one look at the newcomer and began to dance with him.

Bagheera tried to grab Mowgli, but each time, right before he could, one of the monkeys would whirl the boy away from him.

By the time Baloo and Bagheera were finally able to get Mowgli away from King Louie and the monkeys, the ancient ruins had crumbled entirely around the King and his monkey court!

That night, while Mowgli slept, Bagheera explained to Baloo that Shere Khan was after the Man-cub. He convinced Baloo that Mowgli was not safe in the jungle.

The next morning, Baloo reluctantly told Mowgli, 'I've got to take you to the Man-village.'

Hurt and disappointed, Mowgli ran off – only to run into Kaa!

Shere Khan heard that Mowgli had run off and prowled through the jungle looking for the Man-cub. When he heard Kaa singing to someone up in a tree he called the snake down to ask him who was in his coils.

Kaa did not want to share the Man-cub, so he told Shere Khan he was singing to himself.

While Shere Khan and Kaa were talking, Mowgli managed to escape from the snake's coils. He ran off into the jungle once more, feeling more alone than ever before.

Mowgli arrived at a place in the jungle where there was very little grass on the ground and no leaves on the trees. He was soon joined by four vultures.

At first, the vultures tried to tease Mowgli. 'He's got legs like a stork,' one vulture said.

'But he doesn't have any feathers,' said another. All the vultures laughed until they saw how sad Mowgli was.

The vultures tried to cheer Mowgli up. They told him they'd like to make him an honorary vulture. When Mowgli said he'd rather be on his own, they wouldn't take no for an answer. They insisted on singing a friendship song to him. Mowgli began to smile, and soon he was clapping along as the birds continued to sing.

Shere Khan overheard the singing and went over to Mowgli and the vultures.

'Bravo! Bravo!' he said to the vultures when they finished their song. 'And thank you for detaining my victim.'

The vultures were frightened and flew off. From the safety of a tree, they urged Mowgli to run.

But Mowgli turned to Shere Khan and said, 'You don't scare me.'

Mowgli refused to run from the tiger. Shere Khan counted to ten and then leaped at Mowgli, roaring, with all his claws out and his mouth wide open! Baloo arrived in the nick of time and pulled Shere Khan's tail so hard, the tiger fell short of the Man-cub.

The vultures, Mowgli and Baloo all fought against Shere Khan. The tiger ran off when a lightning storm caused a tree to burst into flames and Mowgli tied a burning branch to his tail!

Baloo lay injured and still on the ground. Finally, he opened his eyes and lifted his head. Overjoyed, Mowgli ran and sprang into his friend's arms.

Baloo, Bagheera and Mowgli set off into the jungle once again, and at long last, they reached the Man-village. Mowgli climbed a tree to get a good look at a girl he heard singing down by a watering hole. He couldn't take his eyes off her, to Bagheera's great delight. When the girl saw Mowgli, she smiled shyly at him.

The girl dropped her jug and it rolled to where Mowgli stood. He picked up the jug and followed the girl to the Man-village. He turned around to give Baloo and Bagheera a big, goofy grin.

'Mowgli is where he belongs now,' said Bagheera.

'I think you're right,' said Baloo, and he and Bagheera danced happily back into the jungle.